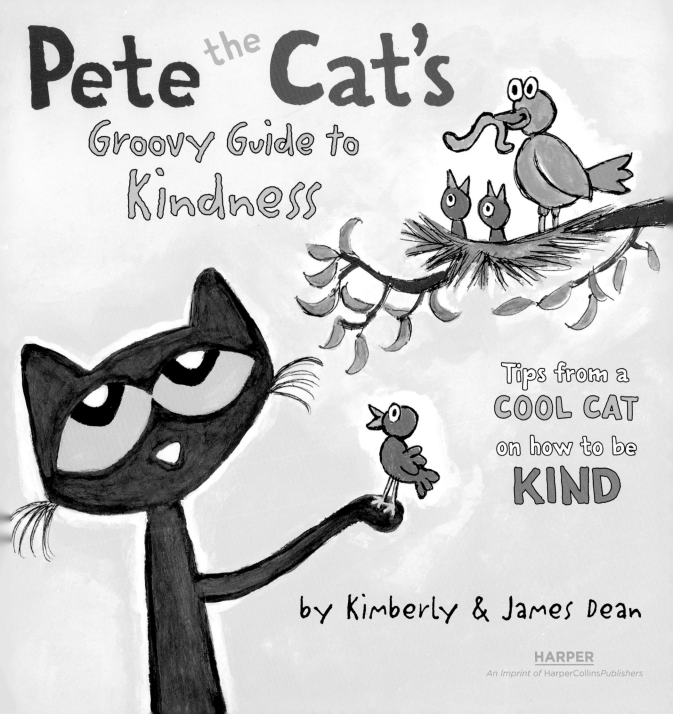

Pete the Cat's
Groovy Guide to Kindness

Tips from a
COOL CAT
on how to be
KIND

by Kimberly & James Dean

HARPER
An Imprint of HarperCollins Publishers

ISBN 978-0-06-297402-0

The artist used pen and ink, with watercolor and acrylic paint, on
300lb hot press paper to create the illustrations for this book.
Typography by Jeanne L. Hogle
20 21 22 23 24   PC   10 9 8 7 6 5 4 3 2

First Edition

For my lifelong mentor, Dr. Wayne Dyer, who said, "When you have the choice
between being right and being kind, choose to be kind."
Ephesians 4:32
—K.D.

"Three things in human life are important: the first is to be kind; the second is to be kind; and the third is to be kind."

—HENRY JAMES

"Guard well within yourself that treasure, kindness. Know how to give without hesitation, how to lose without regret, how to acquire without meanness. **"**

—GEORGE SAND

"No act of kindness, no matter how small, is ever wasted."

—AESOP

"Remember that the happiest people are not those getting more, but those giving more. "

—H. JACKSON BROWN JR.

" for whoever, in enjoying a kindness, knows how to return one as well— he is a friend more valuable than any possession. "

—SOPHOCLES

"Wherever there is a human being, there is an opportunity for kindness."

—LUCIUS ANNAEUS SENECA

"And above all these put on love, which binds everything together in perfect harmony."

—COLOSSIANS 3:14

"Those who are happiest are those who do the most for others. "

—BOOKER T. WASHINGTON

"Try to be a rainbow in someone's cloud."

—MAYA ANGELOU

Integrity is doing the right thing even when no one is watching. "

—UNKNOWN

"Have you had a kindness shown? Pass it on.

—HENRY BURTON

"One kind word can warm three winter months."

—JAPANESE PROVERB

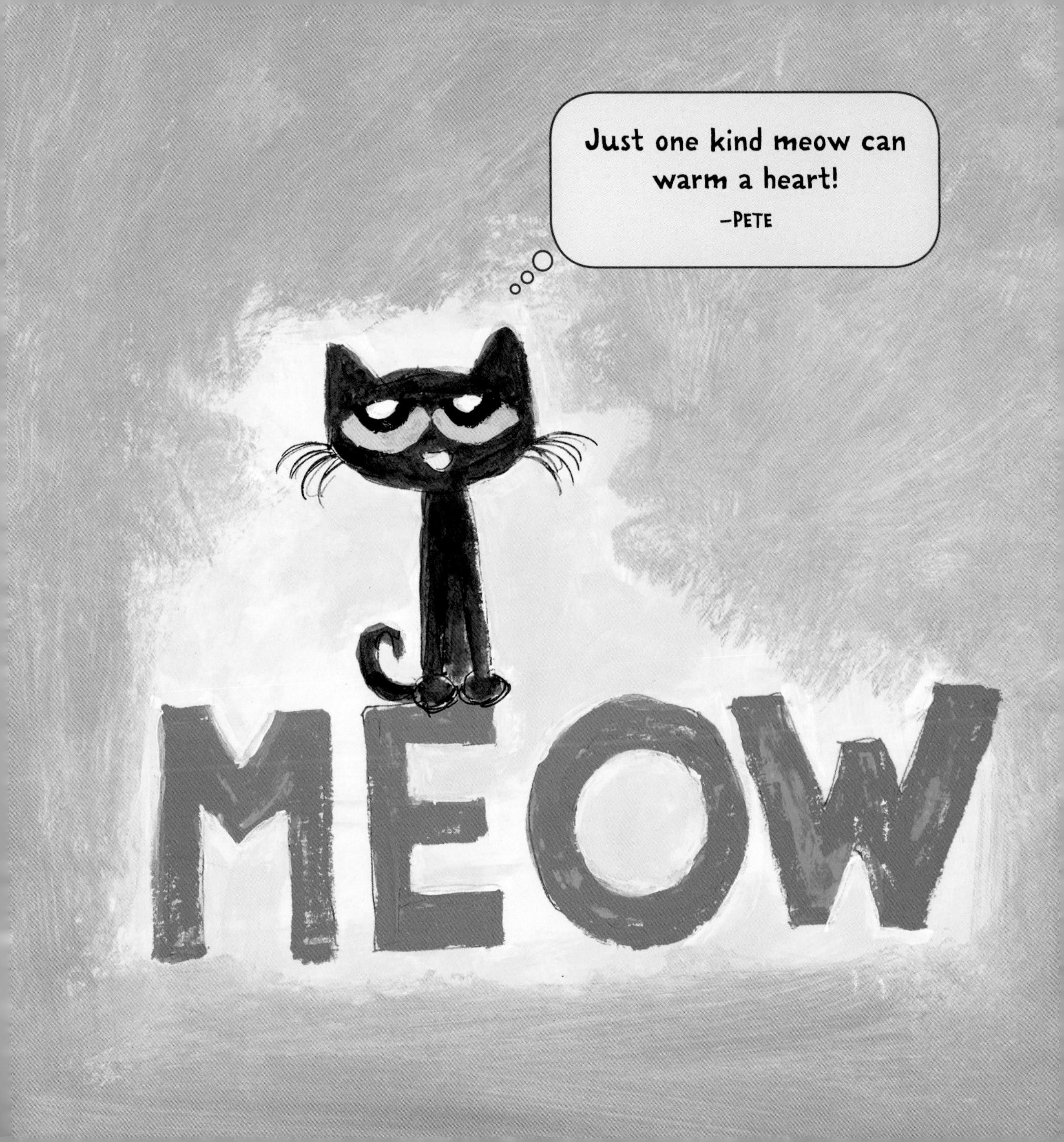
Just one kind meow can warm a heart!
—PETE
MEOW

"Be the change you want to see."

—ATTRIBUTED TO MAHATMA GANDHI

"Kindness is free. Sprinkle that stuff everywhere."

—UNKNOWN

"Be a little kinder
than you have to."

—E. LOCKHART

"It's cool to be kind."

—UNKNOWN

"Our fingerprints don't fade from the lives we touch."

—JUDY BLUME

"friends show their love in times of trouble."

—EURIPIDES

"Be kind whenever possible.
It is always possible."

—DALAI LAMA XIV

"On that best portion of a good man's life; his little, nameless, unremembered acts of kindness and love."

—WILLIAM WORDSWORTH

66Kindness is the touch of an angel's hand.**99**

—JAMES L. GORDON

"Kind people are the best kind of people."

—UNKNOWN

"Never believe that a few caring people can't change the world. For, indeed, that's all who ever have. "

—MARGARET MEAD

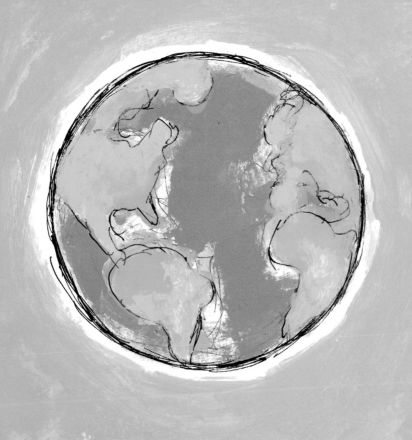

"Kind hearts are the gardens,
kind thoughts are the roots,
kind words are the flowers,
kind deeds are the fruits."

—ENGLISH PROVERB

Kindness grows the coolest flowers!
—PETE